ASPEN COMICS PRESENTS

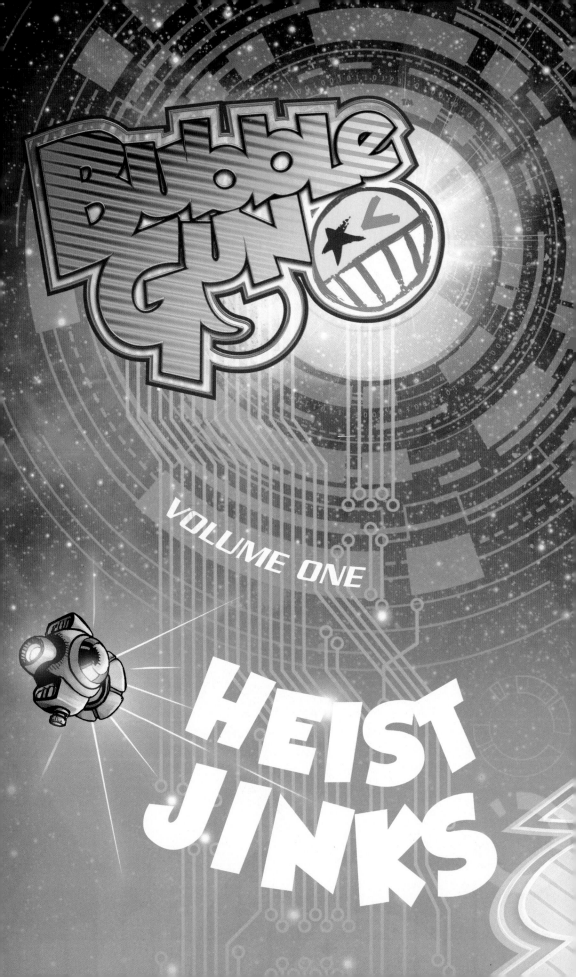

BUBBLEGUN CREATED BY:
MARK ROSLAN

BUBBLEGUN™ VOLUME 1: HEIST JINKS
ISBN: 978-1-941511-15-2 FIRST PRINTING, REGULAR EDITION 2016. *Collects material originally published as BubbleGun 1-5*
ISBN: 978-1-941511-16-9 FIRST PRINTING, COMIC BENTO VARIANT EDITION 2016. *Collects material originally published as BubbleGun*

Published by Aspen MLT, Inc.
Office of Publication: 5701 W. Slauson Ave. Suite 120, Culver City, CA 90230.
The Aspen MLT, Inc. logo® is a registered trademark of Aspen MLT, Inc. BubbleGun™ and the BubbleGun logo are the trademarks of Aspen MLT, Inc. The entire contents of this book, all artwork, characters and their likenesses are © 2016 Aspen MLT, Inc. All Rights Reserved. Any similarities between names, characters, persons, and/or institutions in this publication with persons living or dead or institutions is unintended and is purely coincidental. With the exception of artwork used for review purposes, none of the contents of this book may be reprinted, reproduced or transmitted by any means or in any form without the express written consent of Aspen MLT, Inc.
PRINTED IN THE U.S.A.

Address correspondence to:
BUBBLEGUN *c/o Aspen MLT Inc.*
5701 W. Slauson Ave. Suite 120
Culver City, CA. 90230-6946
or fanmail@aspencomics.com

Visit us on the web at:
aspencomics.com
aspenstore.com
facebook.com/aspencomics
twitter.com/aspencomics

ORIGINAL SERIES EDITORS:
VINCE HERNANDEZ AND FRANK MASTROMAURO
ASSISTANT EDITOR: **JOSH REED**

FOR THIS EDITION:
SUPERVISING EDITOR: **FRANK MASTROMAURO**
EDITORS: **VINCE HERNANDEZ, ANDREA SHEA AND GABE CARRASCO**
COVER DESIGN: **MARK ROSLAN**
BOOK DESIGN AND PRODUCTION: **MARK ROSLAN**
LOGO DESIGN: **PETER STEIGERWALD AND MARK ROSLAN**
REGULAR COVER ILLUSTRATION: **MIKE BOWDEN, MARK ROSLAN AND DAVID CURIEL**
COMIC BENTO COVER ILLUSTRATION: **MARK BROOKS**

FOR ASPEN:
FOUNDER: **MICHAEL TURNER**
CO-OWNER: **PETER STEIGERWALD**
CO-OWNER/PRESIDENT: **FRANK MASTROMAURO**
VICE PRESIDENT/EDITOR IN CHIEF: **VINCE HERNANDEZ**
VICE PRESIDENT/DESIGN AND PRODUCTION: **MARK ROSLAN**
EDITORIAL ASSISTANTS: **GABE CARRASCO AND JOSH REED**
PRODUCTION ASSISTANT: **CHAZ RIGGS**
OFFICE COORDINATOR: **MEGAN MADRIGAL**
AspenStore.com: **CHRIS RUPP**

To find the Comic Sho
nearest you...
888-COMIC-BOOK
csls.diamondcomics.com
1-888-266-4226

Finders, Keepers

chapter ONE

No More Fun

chapter Two

I'M NOT SURE IF I BELIEVE HIM.

I BELIEVE... THAT'S ALL THE MONEY HE HAS, AND WE CAN GET MORE IF WHAT HE'S SAYING IS TRUE.

ROMAN!

THIS IS A LIFE WE'RE TALKING ABOUT. WE CAN'T TREAT IT--

--HIM, ASHER, LIKE OUR USUAL MONEY-FOR-DOCUMENTS TYPE THING.

DEVYN. MAYBE YOU COULD TRY TO SYNC UP WITH HIM TO SEE IF IT'S ALL TRUE. I MEAN... I KNOW IT'S ALWAYS RISKY INTERFACING HUMAN TO HUMAN, BUT-- A COMPUTER THAT ALTERS DNA?

HMM. I ADMIT I'M CURIOUS. WHAT DO YOU THINK, ZUSE?

I CAN'T MAKE THIS DECISION FOR YOU, BUT I WILL SAY TWO THINGS. I'M DYING TO KNOW TOO... BUT REMEMBER...

...CURIOSITY KILLED THE CAT.

I THINK WE'D ALL LIKE TO KNOW. KYO...?

FOR ALL THE TROUBLE WE WENT THROUGH-- YEAH, LET'S DO IT.

IT'S SETTLED THEN. I'LL HAVE TO MANUALLY CONNECT.

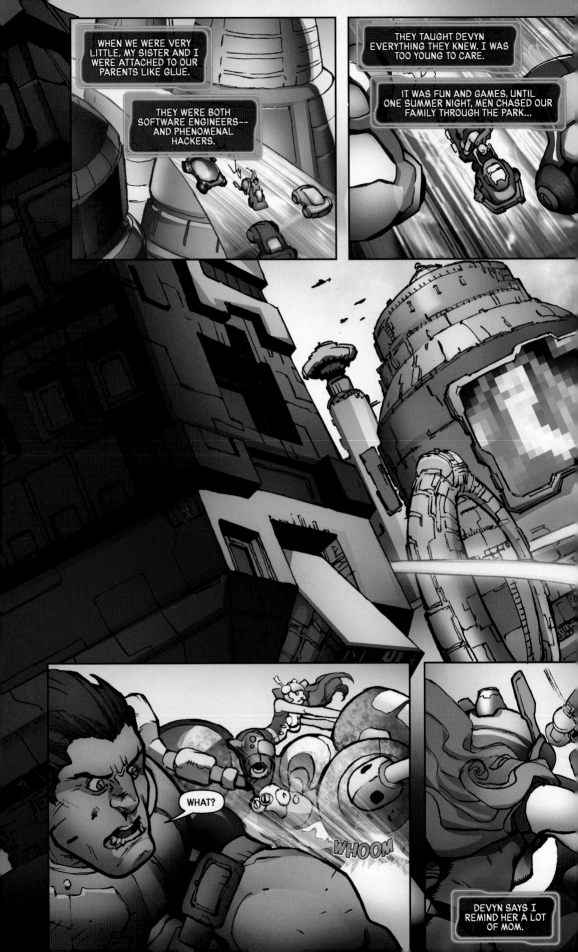

THIS IS ONE HELL OF DAY, ISN'T IT?

WHAT'S WRONG WITH YOU?! HOW COULD YOU BETRAY US?

YOU WON'T SHOOT. I KNOW YOU. YOU'RE NOT A KILLER.

I CAN TEACH YOU HOW TO BE. JOIN ME.

YOUR SISTER IS A SMALL-TIMER. LEAVE THEM BEHIND.

JOIN YOU? YOU'VE CLEARLY TAKEN INSANE-O PILLS. DON'T YOU GIVE A & ABOUT ANYONE OTHER THAN YOURSELF?

WHAT THE BOY IS CAPABLE OF IS JUST TOO DAMN VALUABLE TO SPLIT FIVE WAYS. I CALLED CAINE BACK ON MY OWN AND VITADRONE OFFERED ME EIGHT BILLION. JOIN ME.

I'D RATHER DIE.

HAVE IT YOUR WAY.

TTSSSHHH
BLEEP

FOR F@@K'S SAKE!

~~DEVYN'S~~ MOLLI'S TOP RULE: WHEN THE TIMER HITS ZERO...

BLEEP BLEEP BLEEP

...PRAY.

RA-BOOOOOM

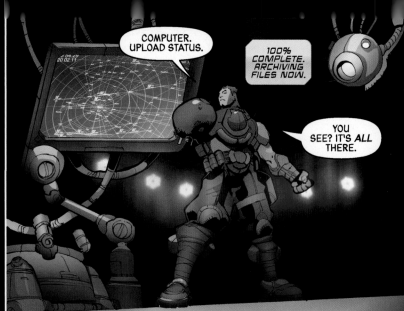

COMPUTER. UPLOAD STATUS.

100% COMPLETE. ARCHIVING FILES NOW.

YOU SEE? IT'S *ALL* THERE.

GREAT JOB, ROMAN. BUT BETRAYAL TO YOUR TEAM WAS A WASTE. YOU'RE MISSING THE BOY.

WHAT MY ASSOCIATE CRAINE MEANS IS, IT'S NOT THE DATA BUT THE BOY HIMSELF THAT'S IMPORTANT. THE DATA IS USELESS WITHOUT HIM.

I DON'T UNDERSTAND. I HAVE EVERYTHING HE WAS HOLDING. EVERYTHING YOU ASKED FOR!

I HAVEN'T FAILED YET. I CAN STILL BE USEFUL. I'LL GET THE BOY.

THAT'S MY JOB NOW. UNLESS THAT'S A PROBLEM FOR YOU. HMM?

NO. NO, IT'S NOT. ATTACK AT WILL.

CRAINE. LEAVE FOR THE BOY NOW. WE'RE LOSING TIME.

ROMAN. YOUR WORK WITH US ISN'T DONE. I'LL NEED YOUR HELP TO BRING ABOUT A CHANGE TO THIS WORLD.

ONE THAT WILL CHANGE IT ALL.

Bellicosity

chapter THREE

I KNOW YOU CO-CREATED AND RUN VITADRONE, ONE OF THE LARGEST MULTI-BILLION WORLDNOTE CORPORATIONS EVER CREATED. "AS HUMANITY MOVES BOLDLY INTO THE FUTURE--"

"--VITADRONE WILL BE LEADING THE WAY."

THAT'S WHAT I'D EXPECT YOU TO KNOW. BUT ROMAN, I'D LIKE YOU TO KNOW MORE. TO BECOME A CONFIDANT. AND MORESO... A FRIEND.

"YEARS AGO, I LOST A CONTRACT TO A COMPETING COMPANY, *TRINION*. THEY INFILTRATED MY PERSONAL SYSTEM WITH HIRED HACKERS, NOT UNLIKE YOU.

"I LEARNED THE HARD WAY THAT BIO-COMPUTATION TECHNOLOGY IS A VERY COMPETITIVE FIELD. THEY KILLED THE LOVE OF MY LIFE, SIMPLY BECAUSE SHE WAS IN THE WAY.

IN MY FIFTEEN YEARS WITH THE COMPANY, I'VE OVERSEEN THE FIRM'S RISE FROM A FEISTY START-UP TO A MULTINATIONAL CONGLOMERATE. BUT WE HAD TO GET OUR HANDS DIRTY TO DO THIS. LIKE YOU'VE DONE WITH YOUR OLD FRIENDS.

THIS BOY WILL HELP ME DO JUST THAT.

"TRINION DEFEATED ME THAT NIGHT. BUT I CRAWLED BACK. I SHOWED THEM I WILL TAKE OUT EACH AND EVERY COMPETITOR THAT STANDS IN VITADRONE'S WAY, NO MATTER WHAT IT TAKES. DO YOU UNDERSTAND?"

HE'S A GAME CHANGER. A CURE TO THE GROWING GERMS OF MANKIND. WITH HIM I CAN IMPERSONATE WHO I WANT, INFILTRATE WHERE I WANT. *DELETE* WHO I WANT.

I CAN BE ANYONE AND ANYWHERE.

I'D STILL LOVE TO BE ME, OF COURSE. AND YOU... I CAN REGROW YOUR ARM IF YOU'D LIKE. YOU COULD BECOME MY PROXY.

AND ONE DAY SOON, VITADRONE WILL BE ABLE TO CROSSBREED MY ADVANCED SYNTHEZOIDS WITH MEN, CREATING AN ARMY OF LOYAL MAN-O-BOTS!

I NEED A MAN LIKE YOU BY MY SIDE. I PERSONALLY CHOSE YOU TO HELP ME LEAD THEM.

SO TELL ME, ROMAN... ARE YOU WITH ME, BROTHER?

YES! I'M WITH YOU. THE *WINNING SIDE.*

THIS WHOLE DAMN WORLD IS A MESS. TOGETHER WE WILL BRING TO IT *ORDER.*

CRAINE WAS WILLING TO KILL US ALL FOR HIM. A LIVING PROGRAM THAT MANIPULATES DNA. *SO WHAT?* CRAINE'S BOSS WANTS TO LOSE SOME WEIGHT?

MAYBE ASHER CAN TAP INTO *MY DNA* AND HEAL ME QUICKER.

IF HE COULD CHANGE *ME,* I'D HAVE HIM MAKE ME A LOT MORE LIKE DEVYN. BEAUTIFUL AND TALL.

YOU CAN'T BE SERIOUS. I WOULDN'T CHANGE A THING ABOUT YOU.

MOLLI, YOU SEEM TO HOLD YOURSELF TO SOME IMPOSSIBLE STANDARD. YOU'RE EVERY BIT AS GREAT AS YOUR SISTER.

I WISH I COULD BELIEVE THAT.

ASHER IS A SCARY IDEA, DON'T YOU THINK, ZUSE? THE WORLD DOESN'T NEED A DNA CHANGER IF YOU ASK ME. HIS TECHNOLOGY IS GETTING INTO TERRITORY THAT SHOULDN'T BE MESSED WITH.

I THINK WE SHOULD CONSIDER DESTROYING HIM.

NO-- WAIT. THAT'S IT! WE CAN'T KILL HIM. ASHER IS TOO VALUABLE.

WE HAVE HIM AND *EVERYONE* WANTS HIM.

A TRADE.

EXACTLY.

ASHER THE CYBER-BOY FOR DEVYN.

SORRY, THEON. IT'S THE ONLY WAY.

LET'S WRAP THIS UP QUICKLY, SHALL WE CRAINE?

IT'S A SHAME THINGS DIDN'T WORK OUT DIFFERENTLY BETWEEN US. TO BE FAIR, WE *DID* MAKE A GENEROUS OFFER.

I'D LIKE TO OFFER A *NEW* PROPOSITION. I NEED TO RECONNECT ASHER AND DEVYN TO WAKE MY SISTER'S CONSCIOUSNESS. IF YOU ALLOW THIS, WE WILL RUN TWO JOBS FOR YOU. NO QUESTIONS ASKED.

INTERESTING. WHILE I COULD USE YOUR SERVICES... I JUST DON'T THINK YOU'RE THE *RIGHT* WOMAN FOR THE JOB. HOW ABOUT THIS... I REBOOT YOUR SISTER FOR YOU...

...BUT I JUST KEEP THEM BOTH.

HAHAHA. SMART CHOICE, GIRLY.

LET HER GO. THE POLICE ARE ON THEIR WAY.

I SAID STAND DOWN, CRAINE. TO THE SHIP... *NOW*.

WE HAVE WHAT WE NEED. BESIDES... SHE'S ALREADY BROKEN.

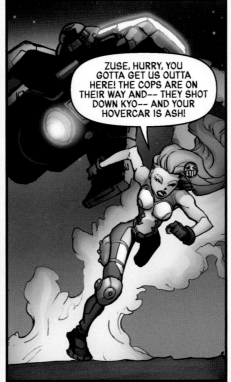

ZUSE, HURRY, YOU GOTTA GET US OUTTA HERE! THE COPS ARE ON THEIR WAY AND-- THEY SHOT DOWN KYO-- AND YOUR HOVERCAR IS ASH!

KYO WAS SHOT? WHAT--?!

I-- I DON'T KNOW. THEY FIRED A ROCKET AT HIM AND--

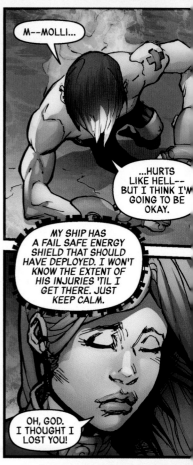

THIS IS ALL TOO MUCH. IT'S LIKE, JUST WHEN EVERYTHING IS GOING GREAT, IT HAS TO TURN FOR THE WORST. WITHOUT FAIL. NEVER THOUGHT THINGS WOULD EVER GET THIS BAD.

THEY TOOK ASHER.

KYO, I'VE LOST DEVYN, BUT I CAN'T LOSE YOU TOO.

YOU'RE NOT GOING TO LOSE ME. I'M FINE. I'M RIGHT HERE. I'VE ALWAYS BEEN RIGHT HERE.

I'LL ALWAYS HAVE YOUR BACK. I'LL ALWAYS LOOK AFTER YOU. BUT NOT JUST AS A TEAMMATE, OR FRIEND, BUT--

MOLLI, I'M NOT SURE HOW TO TELL YOU THIS... AND IT'S NOT THE BEST TIME, BUT--

--CAN YOU STOP TALKING AND-- HOLD ME, KYO-- FOR JUST A LITTLE BIT?

YOU KNOW I WOULDN'T BE HERE IF I DIDN'T ABSOLUTELY HAVE TO BE. SO YES...

...A JOB OF YOUR CHOOSING, NO QUESTIONS ASKED, IN EXCHANGE FOR *THE DARK LIGHTNING.*

FOUR DAYS. THAT'S ALL I NEED. I'LL EVEN WASH HER FOR YOU.

THE DARK LIGHTNING IS NO ORDINARY *SHIP.* SHE'S LIKE MY CHILD. AND YOU DON'T HURT SIR PENNY'S CHILDREN. ONE SCRATCH ON HER AND I SCRATCH BACK.

WILL YOU BE DOING THE SCRATCHING YOURSELF...

...OR DO YOUR ALLEY CATS DO ALL THE DIRTY WORK FOR YOU?

KRAK

BEEP
BEEP

ZUSE. YOU SHOULD BE PATCHED IN. PUT THESE PIGS IN THE DARK.

ALREADY ON IT. CAMERAS DOWN AND WORKING ON THE SECURITY.

I NEED HOLDING CELL SIXTEEN OPEN PRONTO!

SHOULDN'T BE BUT A MOMENT MORE. THE POLICE REALLY NEED TO INVEST IN SOME BETTER SERVERS.

IT'S GETTING VERY HOT OUTSIDE, MOLLI. MOVE QUICKER!

WELL, LOOK WHO IT IS.

WHAT'S GOIN' ON?!

HAVING FUN PLAYING DRESS UP, MOLLI?

THERE IS NO TIME TO EXPLAIN. I'VE COME TO GET YOU THREE OUTTA HERE.

WE'RE NOT GOING ANYWHERE WITH *YOU*.

LOOK, I KNOW WE'VE NEVER LIKED EACH OTHER, BUT I NEED YOU, OKAY--!? I NEED YOUR TEAM'S HELP TO SAVE MY SISTER AND I'M NOT TAKING *NO* FOR AN ANSWER.

WHY SHOULD WE HELP YOU?

IN EXCHANGE, I'M OFFERING YOUR FREEDOM AND THREE BILLION WORLDNOTES, BUT WE HAVE TO MOVE NOW!

MY TEAM'S FREEDOM, *FOUR* BILLION, AND YOU BUY US NEW GEAR OR NO DEAL.

NO JAIL *AND THREE BILL?* COUNT ME IN.

COUNT OLEG IN, TOO.

F/#*ING FINE! NOW MOVE YOUR ASSES!

DEVYN... YOU'RE SUPPOSED TO BE HERE TO HELP ME GET THEON'S SON BACK.

HEY, MOLLI.

LET ME ASK YOU SOMETHING. HOW DID IT FEEL TO WEAR YOUR SISTER'S SUIT?

I BET IT FELT GREAT, HUH? SAME SIZE ALMOST? TEMPORARY CLOAKING ABILITY. I'D LOVE TO HAVE THAT.

BUT IT'S NOT THE SUIT YOU WEAR THAT MAKES YOU WHO YOU ARE.

IT'S WHO YOU ARE UNDERNEATH THAT MATTERS.

LOOK. YOU'RE A BRIGHT GIRL, BUT... I DON'T KNOW IF YOU HAVE WHAT IT TAKES TO GET THROUGH THIS MISSION. THOSE ARE BIG SHOES TO FILL.

WITH DEVYN NOT IN THE SUIT, I'LL FEEL BETTER IF WE RUN WITH *MY* PLAN.

DON'T GET ME WRONG. MY TEAM IS WITH YOU. HELL, THIS MIGHT EVEN BE FUN. BUT SO WE'RE CLEAR, IT'S *STRICTLY* FOR THE MONEY... AND OF COURSE A THANKS FOR OUR FREEDOM.

IT'S JUST BEST IF YOU FOLLOW MY LEAD...

...IF YOU WANT TO SAVE THE CYBER-BOY AND SEE YOUR SISTER AGAIN.

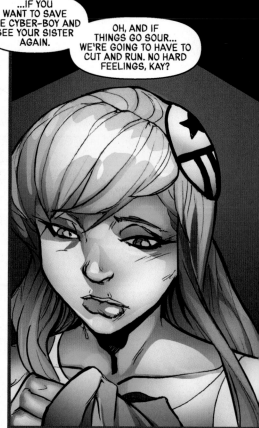

OH, AND IF THINGS GO SOUR... WE'RE GOING TO HAVE TO CUT AND RUN. NO HARD FEELINGS, KAY?

Phaseout

chapter

FIVE

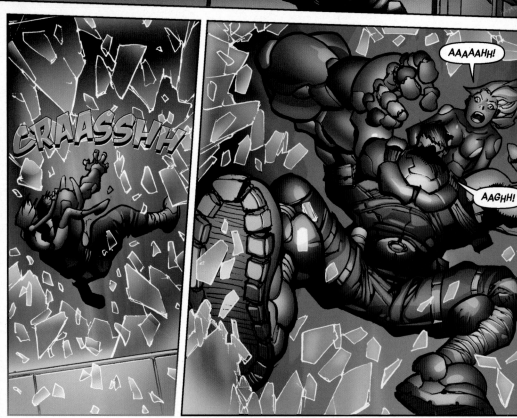

I MUST CONFESS. I'M *COMPLETELY PREPARED* FOR YOUR ARRIVAL, MOLLI. MISDIRECTION-- YOUR TEAM'S SIGNATURE MOVE. ROMAN INFORMED US.

YOU THINK YOU'VE FIGURED US OUT? YOU HAVE *NO IDEA* WHAT WE'RE CAPABLE OF!

I SPARED YOUR LIFE IN THE PARK. IT WAS A *GIFT*-- YOU SHOULD HAVE LEFT US ALONE AND GIVEN UP ON YOUR SISTER. WE NEEDED HER, YOU SEE, TO MAKE ASHER FULLY FUNCTIONAL AGAIN.

HE'S ELPING ME PGRADE MY YNTHEZOIDS. ALTERING THEIR DNA.

TURNING THEM INTO WEAPONIZABLE BIO-DRONES THE LIKES OF WHICH THIS WORLD HAS NEVER SEEN... AN ARMY OF LOYAL CYBORGS!

HOW ABOUT A TEST RUN?

SHWOOO

KA-SPLAM

I COULDN'T KILL HIM.

NOT EVEN CRAINE DESERVES TO DIE.

IT ISN'T IN ME, AND I'M FINE WITH THAT.

HEH. WELL DONE.

KYO! THANK GOD YOU'RE ALIVE!

I *KNEW* YOU COULD DO IT.

I KNOW... YOU'VE *ALWAYS* BELIEVED IN ME.

WOW.

DOES THIS MEAN-- ARE WE... TOGETHER?

LET'S NOT RUSH THINGS AND SEE WHERE IT TAKES US.

WAIT-- WHAT DOES THAT MEAN--?

WHAT DOES SHE MEAN? WHAT DOES SHE MEAN?!

BE COOL, KYO!

HOW LONG WAS I OUT?

DEVYN! YOU'RE AWAKE!

ASHER FIXED ME. THE TWO OF US WERE CONNECTED THE WHOLE TIME. I COULD MAKE OUT THINGS HERE AND THERE, BUT ONE THING WAS CLEAR-- YOU'VE SEEN OUR DARKEST DAY AND SURVIVED IT. WITH SOME HELP, I SEE.

THANK YOU FOR SAVING ME, MOLLI.

JUST FOLLOWING WHAT YOU TAUGHT ME, SIS.

SO-- WAS IT YOU WHO STOPPED THE BIO-DRONES FROM CUTTING US DOWN?

NO. IT WASN'T ME--

--IT WAS ME.

DRAZIC FORCED ME TO HELP BUILD THEM BUT DEVYN AWAKENED M HUMAN SUBCONSCIOUS. I ABLE TO TAP INTO VITADRO SYSTEM AGAIN AND DESTR THEIR PROGRAMMING.

ASHER! WE HAVE TO CALL YOUR FATHER, THEON!

NO--!

ASHER AND I GOT TO KNOW EACH OTHER VERY WELL WHILE WE CONNECTED. WE CAN NOT TAKE HIM TO HIS FATHER.

HE IS NOT WHO HE SAYS HE IS.

AS MUCH AS I'D LIKE TO SOAK IN THIS MOMENT, WE CAN'T STAY.

THE F.B.I. DEFINITELY THEIR WA

COVER GALLERY